02 1176

IRVIN L. YOUNG MEMORIAL LIBRARY
WHITEWATER, WISCONSIN
3488 00130 5471

W9-BXY-854

DATE DUE

GAYLORD PRINTED IN U.S.A.

Mama's Little Bears

by Nancy Tafuri

SCHOLASTIC PRESS • NEW YORK

Irvin L. Young Memorial Library
Whitewater, Wisconsin

T++

One spring day,
Little Bears were fishing
with their Mama.

Little Bears
fished and fished . . .

until . . .

off they ran!

What's over there?

What's under here?

What's in there?

What's down here?

What's up there?

Little Bears
scurried
up,
up,
up.

OH!

Little Bears
hurried
down,
down,
down.

MAMA!

And there she was!

Little Bears hugged
their Mama so tight . . .

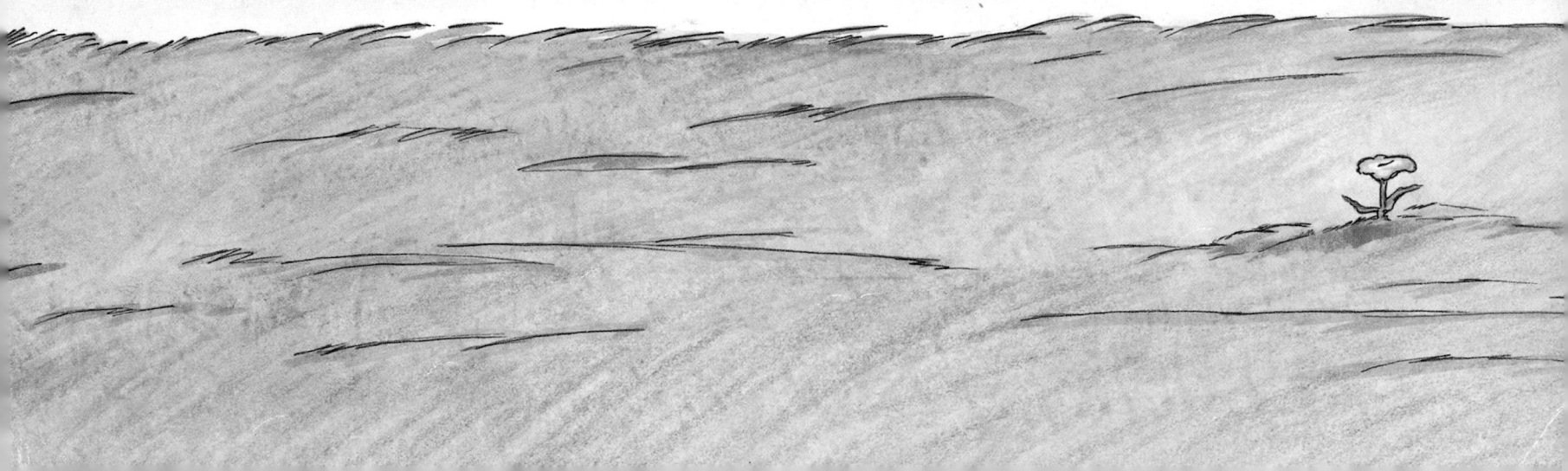

and Mama Bear hugged them right back!

Copyright © 2002 by Nancy Tafuri
All rights reserved. Published by Scholastic Press, a division of Scholastic Inc., *Publishers since 1920.*
SCHOLASTIC, SCHOLASTIC PRESS and associated logos are trademarks and/or registered trademarks of Scholastic Inc.

No part of this publication may be reproduced, or stored in a retrieval system, or transmitted in any form or by any means, electronic, mechanical, photocopying, recording, or otherwise, without written permission of the publisher. For information regarding permission, write to Scholastic Inc., Attention: Permissions Department, 555 Broadway, New York, NY 10012.

LIBRARY OF CONGRESS CATALOGING-IN-PUBLICATION DATA
Tafuri, Nancy.
Mama's Little Bears / by Nancy Tafuri.— 1st ed. p. cm.
Summary: The Little Bears explore their forest home but never stray too far from their Mama.
ISBN 0-439-27311-0 [1.Bears–Fiction. 2. Mother and child–Fiction.] I. Title.
PZ7.T117 Mam 2002 [E]--dc21 2001020935

10 9 8 7 6 5 4 3 2 1 02 03 04 05 06
Printed in Singapore 46 First edition, April 2002

Nancy Tafuri's art was rendered in watercolor paint and pastels. The text type was set in 54-point Garamond Three.
The display type was set in Goudy Handtooled. Book design by Nancy Tafuri and David Saylor

For Cristina

Irvin L. Young Memorial Library
Whitewater, Wisconsin